KU-269-387

This book belongs to

Happiness   Wisdom

....

Cocoa   Beauty Sleep

This is the story of Crystal Clean,

the sleeping daughter of a king and queen.

On every page, can you guess what?

There's a feather duster for you to spot.

Sleeping Beauty

Nick and Claire Page

Illustrations by Sara Baker

make
believe
ideas

Once a king and queen
held a party on the green,
to celebrate their baby.
They called her Crystal Clean.

They were thrilled to bits!
The king did the splits.
The queen served lots of crackers
with lots of cheesy bits.

7

Among the many guests
to welcome the princess
were seven kindly fairies,
who came with presents to bless.

A scary fairy came.
Griselda was her name.
She hadn't been invited
but walked in all the same.

"A curse!" Griselda said.
"A curse upon her head!
She'll be stabbed by a spindle.
Your baby will be dead!"

"No need for any fears,"
the youngest fairy cheers.
"I'll change this curse, instead
she will sleep for a hundred years."

Cocoa

Beauty Sleep

The queen warns Crystal Clean,
each year till she's sixteen,
"Don't ever touch a spindle.
You don't know where it's been."

14

But then one night,
much to her delight,
the princess found a secret tower,
and there, shining bright . . .

15

a spinning wheel she found,
spinning round and round.
She pricked her little finger
and fell to the ground.

DO NOT TOUCH

You couldn't hear a peep.
Everybody fell asleep.
The place was filled with snoring
and dreaming deep.

19

A hundred years went by.
The ivy climbed so high,
you'd never know the castle
stood nearby.

Then along the forest floor,
comes a prince, who finds the door.
He cuts through thorns and roses
and thinks he hears a snore.

WEED
BE GONE

The castle's in a mess.
The prince finds the princess.
He falls in love, he kisses her,
and she wakes up! Success!

23

He marries Crystal Clean,
and on the village green
they hold the biggest party
that you have ever seen!

Ready to tell

Oh no! Some of the pictures from this story have been mixed up! Can you retell the story and point to each picture in the correct order?

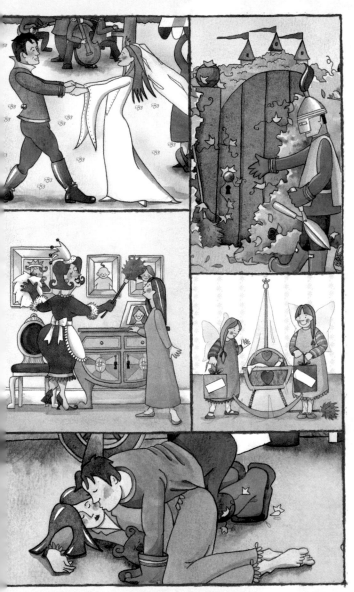

27

Picture dictionary

Encourage your child to read these words from the story and gradually develop his or her basic vocabulary.

castle

fairy

needle

party

presents

pricks

prince

princess

spinning wheel

Key words

Here are some key words used in context. Help
your child to use other words from the border
in simple sentences.

The king **and** queen
have a baby girl.

She will prick her finger.

A prince finds the castle.

He kisses **the** princess.

They hold a big party.

Make a spinning star

You might not have a spinning wheel at home, but you can still weave a colourful woollen star. It's so simple!

You will need
2 sticks of equal length, such as chopsticks or toothpicks • lengths of wool in different colours

What to do
1 Form a cross with the sticks, then use the wool to ti them together, finishing with a knot. Do not cut the w
2 Keeping the wool taut, weave it under and around each stick in turn. The circle will gradually get bigger as you work towards the end of the sticks.
3 Change colours every so often by tying in a new strand of wool whenever you feel like it.
4 Experiment with weaving the wool in and out in different ways.
5 If, when you have finished, you have any gaps, try weaving in lengths of ribbon. You can also try making little shapes out of card or wood and gluing them onto your woollen star.
6 To hang up your star, tie a length of wool through the woven wool at the top of one stick, make a loop, a knot it. Pin up your star and let it spin!